Snoring Beauty

By Sudipta Bardhan-Quallen

Illustrated by Jane Manning

Harper
An Imprint of HarperCollins Publishers

Library of Congress Cataloging-in-Publication Data

Bardhan-Quallen, Sudipta.
    Snoring Beauty / by Sudipta Bardhan-Quallen ; illustrated by Jane Manning. — First edition.
        pages   cm
    Summary: "A new spin on 'Sleeping Beauty' told from the perspective of a little mouse who can't get to sleep
because of the princess's very loud snoring"— Provided by publisher.
    ISBN 978-0-06-087403-2 (hardcover bdgs) — ISBN 978-0-06-087405-6 (lb bdgs)
    [1. Stories in rhyme. 2. Mice—Fiction. 3. Snoring—Fiction. 4. Princesses—Fiction. 5. Characters
in literature—Fiction. 6. Humorous stories.]   I. Manning, Jane, 1960– illustrator.   II. Title.
PZ8.3.B237Sn   2014   2012050669
[E]—dc23   CIP
                                                          AC

The artist used watercolor on Lanaquarelle watercolor paper to create the illustrations for this book.
Typography by Dana Fritts
13 14 15 16 17 SCP 10 9 8 7 6 5 4 3 2 1

First Edition

To B, who snores. And is beautiful
—SBQ

To Kristin, for her
friendship and support
—JKM

THE night before his wedding day,
The skies were dark and dreary.
But in his house,
A little Mouse
Was dreaming of his dearie.

Mouse grinned a goofy little grin,
And settled in for dozing.
He needed rest
To look his best,
But as his eyes were closing . . .

From deep inside the tower room,
  There came a monstrous roaring.
    It shook the night,
    As, tucked in tight,
  Lay Sleeping Beauty . . .
      . . . snoring.

"I know *someday* a prince will come
  To break this spell," Mouse grumbled.
    'Til then, each quake
    Kept Mouse awake
  As Beauty's snoring rumbled.

Mouse rose to close the shutters; then
He peeked outside the tower.
His eyes grew wide.
"A prince!" he cried.
"I'll sleep within the hour!"

"My name is Max," the prince announced,
His manner prim and snooty.
With shoulders squared,
Prince Max declared,
"I'm here for Sleeping Beauty."

Rushing to unlock the gate,
  Mouse welcomed Max, elated.
    From Beauty's room
      Came *SNOOOOGA-SNOOOOOM,*
And Mouse's hopes deflated.

"Who waits in there? A troll? A bear?"
  Asked Max through all the clatter.
    The tower shook.
    From every nook
Small creatures ran and scattered.

"Oh no!" Mouse cried, and quickly lied:
"It's just some creaky flooring.
Go on ahead!
Although," Mouse said,
"She may be *softly* snoring."

But Max was not a bit alarmed—
He said, "I'll do my duty!"
He drew his sword
And hurried toward
The sleeping princess Beauty.

As Max knelt next to Beauty's bed,
Her lashes gently fluttered.
Prince Max leaned in,
Mouse hid a grin,
And then . . .
. . . *HONK-SHOOOOO*, she sputtered.

Prince Max blew back, surprised and shocked.
"Egad! How loud!" he bellowed.
"Oh, rats!" Mouse wept.
Though Beauty slept,
The *GRRRRRR-PFFFFFFF*s
hadn't mellowed.

Mouse said, "Let's work together now
   To stop these royal sputters.
      I propose
      We hold her nose."
"Oh, I suppose," Max muttered.

Mouse waited for a snoring pause,
   Then pinched her nostrils tightly.
      Max puckered up,
      But then, *KER-SCHUPPP!*
She snorted impolitely.

They grabbed two pitchers from a shelf
As Beauty lay *KA-RENCHHHHH*ing.
Mouse yelled, "Heave-ho!"
From high and low
They gave her face a drenching.

Mouse held his breath, Max bit his lip.
"Could this be it?" they wondered.
The room grew still.
No sound, until
SCURRRAAFFFFFA-RAAFFF,
she thundered.

"Let's try another plan," said Mouse,
    "To solve this snoring pickle."
        Max nodded yes.
        Mouse said, "I guess
We *could* give her a tickle."

They pulled the sheets from Beauty's feet,
    And soon they heard her titter.
        But when *ARRRGHOOOOM*
        Boomed through the room
Both Mouse and Max grew bitter.

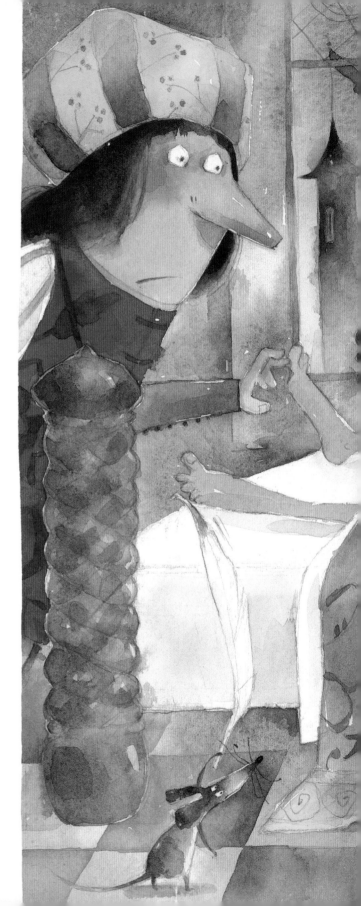

ARRRGHOOOOM

Mouse wrung his hands and stared at Max.
"That's it! I'm done!" Max shouted.
To Mouse's pleas
Of "Kiss her, *please!*"
Prince Max just frowned and pouted.

"I like the crown, I like the throne,
I really like the castle."
Max shook his head.
He shrugged and said,
"The snoring's too much hassle."

As Max walked off, Mouse heard
CARRROOOOOOOSH.
He paced before the mirror.
"One kiss would do!
But how? From who?"
At once . . . it all got clearer.

Mouse knew what he would have to do.
"I hope I won't get cooties!"
Through roaring snores
Mouse crossed the floor,
And pressed his lips to Beauty's.

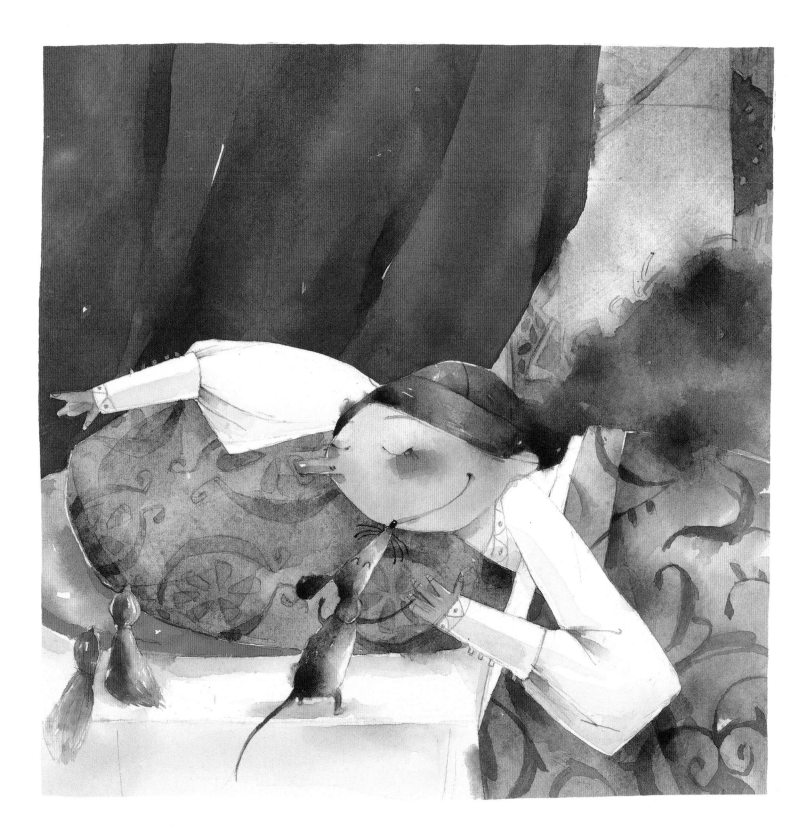

Mouse pulled away and spit—*"Pthoo!"*
   The day's first light was dawning.
      He heard a high
      Yet sleepy sigh —
   And Beauty started yawning!

She rubbed her tired, drowsy eyes—
   A sight Mouse found quite splendid.
      He ran outside
      To Max and cried,
"The snoring finally ended!"

Max followed Mouse into the room.
"Go kiss her now," Mouse prodded.
Max bent a knee,
Said, "Marry me!"
And Beauty beamed and nodded.

With just a bit of time to sleep,
Mouse slumped against his bedding.
He woke at eight
To celebrate
His stylish double wedding.

Mouse kissed his bride and Max kissed his.
They stood together grinning.
Mouse raised his cup
And offered up
A toast to new beginnings.

But when he tried to sleep that night,
Mouse woke to monstrous roaring.
He clutched his ears
And fought back tears,
While Mrs. Mouse . . .

. . . lay snoring.